SPOTLIGHT ON AN EQUITABLE WORLD

DECIDING TO CARE

Mary Ratzer

ROSEN PUBLISHING

Published in 2025 by The Rosen Publishing Group, Inc.
2544 Clinton Street, Buffalo, NY 14224

First Edition

Editor: Greg Roza
Book Design: Michael Flynn

Photo Credits: Cover Dmytro Zinkevych/Shutterstock.com; cover, p. 3 (hands) Dedraw Studio/Shutterstock.com; (series Earth icon) v4ndhira/Shutterstock.com; pp. 5, 22 Ground Picture/Shutterstock.com; p. 6 marekuliasz/Shutterstock.com; p. 7 Michael Spomer/Cal Sport Media/Alamy Live News; p. 9 Iryna Tolmachova/Shutterstock.com; p. 10 shine.graphics/Shutterstock.com; p. 11 Ivan Nikolov/WENN.com/Alamy; p. 13 Portographer/Shutterstock.com; p. 14 Halfpoint/Shutterstock.com; p. 15 Chansom Pantip/Shutterstock.com; p. 17 (main) Tomsickova Tatyana/Shutterstock.com; p. 17 (inset) Sidney de Almeida/Shutterstock.com; p. 18 Jasminko Ibrakovic/Shutterstock.com; p. 19 tolga ildun/Shutterstock.com; p. 21 wavebreakmedia/Shutterstock.com; p. 23 Pressmaster/Shutterstock.com; p. 25 phBodrova/Shutterstock.com; p. 26 F01 PHOTO/Shutterstock.com; p. 27 Viktoriia Hnatiuk/Shutterstock.com; p. 29 i_am_zews/Shutterstock.com.

Cataloging-in-Publication Data

Names: Ratzer, Mary Boyd.
Title: Deciding to care / Mary Ratzer.
Description: Buffalo, NY : Rosen Young Adult, 2025. | Series: Spotlight on an equitable world | Includes glossary and index.
Identifiers: ISBN 9781499477405 (pbk.) | ISBN 9781499477245 (library bound) | ISBN 9781499476965 (ebook)
Subjects: LCSH: Empathy--Juvenile literature. | Apathy--Juvenile literature.
Classification: LCC BF575.E55 R38 2025 | DDC 152.4'1--dc23

Manufactured in the United States of America

Some of the images in this book illustrate individuals who are models. The depictions do not imply actual situations or events.

CPSIA Compliance Information: Batch #CSRYA25. For further information contact Rosen Publishing at 1-800-237-9932.

CONTENTS

Chapter One

BUILDING BLOCKS OF EMPATHY

Caring has the power to transform perspectives, motivation, choices, and actions. Think about the absence of empathy as the starting point. Indifference or apathy are responses that block the possibility of seeing, hearing, understanding, or responding to the needs of another person. Middle and high school students are often part of tightly knit groups that pay attention to popularity, acceptance, and fitting in. When others are targets of negative speech or actions, a young person may protect their own interests and turn their back on empathy. They ignore a problem that is not immediately affecting them. They decide to disconnect rather than to care.

The first step toward caring is awareness and paying attention to other people. That can mean sharing another's positive experience or noticing another student's isolation in a classroom. That can mean listening and considering another's perspective. Paying attention if someone is a target of mean words or hurtful behavior is the next step. Putting yourself in their position and raising your awareness of their situation breaks away from apathy and indifference.

Empathy comes from awareness and understanding of another person's needs, experiences, feelings, or ideas. Feeling the misery of a peer who is physically taunted in a hallway opens a connection that can lead to support. Listening to a person who shares a problem opens a connection that leads to caring and kindness. Empathy is a choice to be an ally. Empathy closes the distance between strangers. Empathy has the power to change our communities for the better.

You can choose to show empathy to others, or you can remain apathetic to others. Which do you think will help build a stronger community?

Chapter Two

EMPATHY IS ITS OWN REWARD

As a young athlete in Nebraska, Malachi Coleman spent most of his life in foster homes. After many difficult years, he and his sister were adopted. They finally experienced a loving home and family. His adoptive mom began to encourage this young man to think about helping others. He rejected all the ideas she suggested, until he agreed to do just one thing for other people. He held doors open for his classmates and teachers. He then held doors open for others wherever and whenever he could. He confided to his mom that he liked doing this because it made him feel good.

His success on the football field in high school won him the opportunity to earn money through sponsorships. He made the decision to use his earnings to help kids in the foster care system. He learned firsthand the emotional and physical effects of being a foster kid, and his personal choice made a difference for young people in the foster care system. His advocacy and personal action for others

Malachi decided to found an organization called Fly Like Chai. It aims to provide opportunities for kids in foster care to explore interests in sports, arts, technology, and education.

was a giant step from indifference to a commitment to be part of the solution. His deep understanding and awareness of the experience of kids like himself motivated and defined his empathetic response.

Empathy taps into the reward center in the brain. Like many other creatures in the animal kingdom, humans who help others feel positive and good about themselves. Winning at video games or getting a positive response from a teacher also tap the reward system. Exercise can do the same. Feeling good about helping another person might have contributed to how humans survived as a species.

Chapter Three

FINDING YOUR BEST SELF

You can find evidence of empathy in many places, just waiting to be noticed. Kindness, caring, generosity, support, and putting the needs of another ahead of one's own are ways people show empathy and find their best selves. They inspire and model choices within anyone's reach.

You can find possibilities for empathy from stories in the media. Examples are easy to find. A cheerleading competition in West Chicago, Illinois, was interrupted when the sound system cut out just as a team started their program. The competing teams stepped up and counted the beats this team needed to finish. Young people who compete are likely to learn empathy for their teammates. They can adapt and extend that social skill to others, even competitors.

Each year, *Time* magazine features a Kid of the Year for their empathy and action to help others. An 11-year-old in Texas named Orion Jean was a finalist in 2022. Jean created "A Race to Kindness," an organization that inspires others to advance kindness. Its initiatives have included providing more than 100,000 meals to people and 500,000 books to kids in need. Sammie Vance, another finalist, started when she was eight years old to work to place buddy benches at her school's playgrounds. These benches would be a place where kids who were feeling alone, as she had at times, could sit to signal this feeling to others, who could then ask them to play. With her mom's help, Sammie worked with the company Green Tree Plastics to have the benches made out of recycled bottle caps.

Sammie's idea has spread! Other schools can host drives for plastic from used items like milk jugs and shampoo bottles to have the company Polywood turn the plastics into Buddy Benches.

Chapter Four

EMPATHY CLOSE TO HOME

You are part of a community. People in your neighborhood, school, town, or city at this exact moment need the support of others. Every day in countless locations, young people just like you are making solutions happen for those who need their help. Kids like you share talents, strengths, and time because they empathize with others in need. Young volunteers use collaboration, planning, and organization to make a difference.

Some empathy close to home grows and extends to thousands of people. On a visit to a shelter with his mom, Nicholas Lowinger noticed that many children there did not have shoes. Some even had to miss school because they took turns with siblings wearing the same pair of shoes. He founded an organization with his family and peers called Gotta Have Sole, eventually supplying 10,000 pairs of shoes to kids who needed them.

Donating your old shoes to shoe drives can reduce clutter in your house and help those in need. Some organizations will pay a lot of money for the collected shoes, which can then be donated to an important cause.

Each year, the Nickelodeon channel celebrates the Halo Awards. These are given to teens who have demonstrated that they care about others in need. Nicholas Lowenger appears on the right.

The Waterford-Halfmoon Union Free School District in Waterford, New York, launched a shoe donation drive for Africa and Central America during their Kindness Month activities. If kids have no shoes in parts of Africa, they cannot go to school. The students at Waterford-Halfmoon repurposed their unused shoes for those in need. Empathy and awareness are engines of positive change like this.

Many similar efforts dot American towns. Eagle Scout projects and capable volunteer groups of kids organize donations of laptops or repair laptops to give to students who cannot afford this essential tool for learning. Food drives, school supply drives, sports equipment drives, winter coat drives, and fundraising efforts have kids as the driving force.

Chapter Five

EMPATHY WINS

You are competing in a cross-country running race or a track event. If you were close to making a really good time or winning, what would you do if a teammate or competitor fell or collapsed? Stopping to assist, you would sacrifice your success in competing. Does the athlete win or does empathy win?

A young high school runner in Alaska, Geremu Daggett, went back to help a teammate who was struggling just a short distance from the finish line. Division finals were a high-stakes competition, but this runner looked back and saw a fellow runner fall. He turned around and pulled his fellow runner across the line.

Abbey D'Agostino of America and Nikki Hamblin of New Zealand were competing in the women's 5,000-meter race when both fell. First Abbey helped Nikki up, who had fallen hard on her shoulder. Later in the race, Abbey, who'd injured her ankle, fell again and Nikki helped her up. Like so many who had trained for years to reach their Olympic dream, they both understood the reasons to make the choice to stop and help. Empathy motivated them. Some would see this as the Olympic spirit.

The media often highlights the runner who helps another runner over the finish line. Rivals do step up and make the other person more important than themselves. Athletes who collapse because of exhaustion or suffer injuries inspire others who know exactly what they are feeling and what they need. Accounts of selfless sportsmanship shine a light on the power of empathy.

Empathy can allow coaches, parents, and teammates to help each other push through tough moments in sport.

Chapter Six

EMPATHY HEROES

Empathy heroes are people who use their talents and strengths to help others. Most of the time these heroes are invisible. Good things happen because of empathy heroes.

Computer Literacy Education Outreach

Students at Canterbury School in Fort Myers, Florida, were joking about their grandparents' struggles with smartphones and tablets. At the nearby Brookdale Senior Living complex, a number of residents struggled to use smartphones for many tasks including texting photos and managing emails. Enthusiastic teens contacted the complex and offered to teach the residents computer literacy. Weekly visits resulted in bonds of friendship and gratitude.

When teens help older people with technology, they can learn important life skills such as patience, emotional intelligence, and communication while helping others avoid social isolation.

Be My Eyes

A person who is blind cannot read or see objects, abilities that most people take for granted. Be My Eyes is a cell phone app that allows a person who is blind to use a cell phone camera to capture what is in front of them. They can then share this image with one of a network of volunteers ready to be their eyes. Volunteers can describe important details and provide amazing access to needed visual information.

Health Care for the Homeless

For 40 years, Boston Doctor Jim O'Connell went out into the city where unhoused men and women spent their nights in tents or on the streets. Connecting with people experiencing homelessness where they were, he provided food, assistance, and medical care. Using an outreach van, he personally earned their trust. He opened Boston Health Care for the Homeless, serving anyone who sought help.

Chapter Seven

EMPATHY IN THE AIR

Airports are fun and exciting for some. However, rushing crowds, unfamiliar sounds, and complications are challenges for everyone. They are extremely challenging for children and adults with special needs, autism spectrum disorder, or anxiety. Understanding how difficult it can be for people with these challenges has inspired a creative and caring response.

American Airlines and other carriers now offer experiences that prepare children and their families for flying. Because autism affects 1 in 36 children and anxiety is common even in adults, practicing the experience of flying and navigating an airport is one way to gain needed support. Families and community organizations that focus on disabilities partner with airline staff to make flying as stress free as possible.

Kids get to practice all the aspects of air travel and reduce the stress of a new experience. From the parking garage to the ticket counter, the security check, and the boarding process, airline staff are helpful guides. Understanding the emotions and the needs of clients with challenges is the starting point for access to travel for all.

Many airports participate in the Hidden Disabilities Sunflower program, offering sunflower lanyards to show airport staff that the person wearing the lanyard has a hidden disability. Those with sensory issues can also take refuge in quiet spaces that have become available in certain airports, such as Boston Logan Airport. The airline staff learn to understand travel difficulties and respond with useful assistance. Awareness of the stress and difficulty of travel for children and adults with special needs leads to solutions and empathy in the air.

Many airlines are offering children with autism and their families the option to pre-board before anyone else. This allows the child to board the plane in a more controlled and less overwhelming environment.

Chapter Eight

RESPONDING TO GLOBAL DISASTERS

Caring about the needs of others can lead to true heroism. Empathy heroes give their talent, strengths, and skills to others with many challenges and even dangers in their paths. Natural disasters happening around the world call for a response to help people. The earthquakes that struck Türkiye and Syria in early 2023 brought rescue teams and all kinds of aid from dozens of countries. Empathy pulled volunteers out of the safety of their lives to face catastrophe.

Members of Virginia Task Force 1 in Fairfax County, Virginia, joined thousands attempting to find and rescue those trapped under the crumpled buildings in Türkiye that used to be homes. With 79 trained volunteers and at least six dogs, they flew to remote disaster-stricken areas far from home. Working in the cold and around the

Teams of trained workers from all over the world rushed to Türkiye in 2023 to help victims of the earthquake. Here, a Japanese health team helps care for those affected by the disaster.

clock, they assisted in the fight against time. Finding survivors in the rubble was in doubt after three days, but the rescue teams used their special skills to save many lives. The human suffering witnessed through the media made millions aware of the crisis. Empathy motivated those not affected by the earthquakes to donate funds for basic needs and medical care for people who lost everything.

Citizens of the places where over 6,000 buildings collapsed needed everything. Shelter, food, warmth, clothing, and medical care are just a few of the needs of those who survived the quakes. World Central Kitchen, Doctors Without Borders, the Red Cross, and countless other organizations exist with the purpose of responding to human needs in times of crisis. Empathy heroes are inspiring models for compassion and action.

Chapter Nine

EMPATHY AND DECISION-MAKERS

Decision-makers and leaders can help build just and caring communities. Respecting the rights, values, hopes, and needs of everyone in the community leads to decisions based on empathy. Building relationships with community members and groups opens a pathway for listening and understanding. The strongest concerns of leaders can be cost and efficiency for their projects. If leaders planned more projects with empathy and awareness for others' emotions, they would build the trust and productivity that can make projects more successful.

Some public agencies are shifting the way decisions are made to better engage with the community. Creating relationships within the community helps leaders recognize the needs of those who live there. Empathy leads to outcomes that solve problems and support equity. For example, empathy can help leaders address common workplace problems, such as distrust and burnout, while helping workers build resilience, or the ability to adjust after major changes.

Leaders often show empathy in schools. Decision-makers paid attention to funding school breakfast and lunch during the COVID-19 pandemic. With many parents out of work, the need to make free meals available solved problems like food insecurity and the effects of hunger on learning. The policy that funded those meals solved a problem with empathy. Some schools even provided two meals a day for kids who were learning remotely by setting up a pickup location for food. That funding stopped in June of 2022 when COVID became less of a problem. Some local schools and state level leaders are working on ways to keep this program running.

Studies show that healthy school breakfast programs help students have better moods during the day, and these programs help students to be more alert.

Chapter Ten

RESPECT AND TRAUMA

A man who wears a T-shirt that reads "Empathy is the answer" oversees a large shelter in Chicago, Illinois. Ryan Dowd inspires and guides those who work with people who are homeless, people with addictions to drugs or alcohol, and victims of trauma. He teaches the skills that lead to respect and human dignity.

Often, the people who need help in a community have experienced stress and anxiety. About 40 percent of students in schools across the United States have experienced enough stress and trauma to be at risk in many ways. Empathy is the answer for them. Maybe they are dealing with poverty or homelessness. Maybe they have been victims of violence. Perhaps they do not have enough food or support within their families. Children could be affected by family instability or

Experiencing homelessness can take a toll on someone's self-worth. Simply smiling and saying hello to someone you see on the street can make a difference, but be sure to also respect their personal space.

Many people donate money to local charities, and that is a good thing. However, people experiencing trauma need more than monetary donations; they need personal contact and empathy.

crisis. Maybe they have lost everything in a fire, flood, or other disaster. Empathy needs to go beyond supplying resources and meeting material needs. Empathy builds trust and rebuilds the human dignity taken away by loss and trauma.

Volunteers can make a huge difference for people in these circumstances. Yet there is more to volunteering than simple actions like providing material items. Volunteers are a lifeline and a source of hope. When people have experienced great stress or have struggled to survive, they need to be understood. They may need an emotional connection, a simple greeting, a smile of welcome, and patience. Working with people who have experienced loss or insecurity requires special knowledge and abilities. But for any volunteer, the best starting point is to have patience, respect, and empathy.

Chapter Eleven

NO EMPATHY HERE

Think about witnessing or even being a part of hurtful, harmful actions in school. Physical, emotional, or social pain can often be a part of someone's school day. Groups of kids can target an individual or another group. Group members act because of negative ideas and attitudes about the targets. Or they decide to randomly act on impulse, sometimes prompted by popular peers, social media, or even rumors.

The teens in a high school record fights and post them on social media. Kids know when fights might happen and gather to watch. A TikTok challenge is causing problems for school staff and students because it encourages students to cause damage in school bathrooms and share their activity online. A girl is assaulted by four others because of a look she gave to someone. Kids are pushed into a status where they cannot walk down a hallway without receiving abusive speech or actions.

To stay in a popular group, kids follow a peer with social power and deliver hateful messages to someone on social media. Even those with empathy for the target can participate to keep their good standing within the popular peer group. Popularity wins out over empathy in this example.

Middle school students have attitudes and ideas about others that can be based on emotional reactions, quick judgments, biases, or assumptions. Because the brains of middle school students are still growing and developing, they may decide a mere look from someone else is a threat or disrespectful. They may react with emotion instead of a responsible decision. As students mature, their decision-making becomes more responsible and reasonable.

Videos on social media platforms such as TikTok are viewed by thousands—sometimes millions—of people all over the world. Cyberbullies can use social media to hurt online victims.

Chapter Twelve

WHEN WE DISCONNECT

Everyone needs acceptance and friends who genuinely care about their well-being. The challenges of fitting in and finding these things can be complicated. This is especially true for young people who are still developing the ability to make safe and smart decisions. Skills needed to manage emotions are also a work in progress. Regulating unkind actions or mean speech can defy social pressures and risk rejection by a clique, group, or circle. A disconnect with empathy takes place.

In person and online, young people often experience anxiety, insecurity, stress, and loss of self-esteem because of mean speech, harassment, and negative interactions with others. Many social media sites require users to be at least 13 years old, but half of 11 to 12 year olds engage in the pressures of fitting in each day online by using

Harassment is when someone's words or actions are so serious that they harm another's well-being and rights. Bullying and harassment can target a person's true or perceived traits including their race, religion, color, ancestry, disability, or gender expression or identity.

TikTok. When a person becomes a target of mean words or actions, there can be pressure to participate. Being on the wrong side of a group expectation can be stressful. It is easier to follow and fit in. Peer pressure wins out and you can make the choice to be mean.

When young people compare themselves to others who are popular or powerful, they might face a decision to follow the lead of a negative role model. Targets of mean behavior, in person or online, are at risk of social isolation and problems with mental health. Empathy for the target encourages the choice to be kind no matter the consequences. Getting in touch with what feels like the right thing to do prompts the right decision.

Chapter Thirteen

WAKE-UP CALL

In 2013 in London, England, a young girl died because of an asthma attack. She lived in an area where low-income families live. Very heavy traffic in that part of the city caused serious air pollution that was a health hazard. For many years, decision-makers delayed action to reduce the health threats due to the cost and effort required.

When Ella Kissi-Debrah died, the coroner said failure to reduce pollution levels to legal limits was a factor in her death. Pollutants in her neighborhood exceeded limits set by the European Union and World Health Organization. Ella's mother had to fight to get experts to testify to the effects of toxic air on Ella and its role in her death. That finally got decision-makers to wake up and act with respect for the people affected by toxic air.

In many U.S. cities, air quality threatens the health and well-being of children and adults living near highways, railroad tracks, factories, and solid waste dump sites. Researchers have proven that air quality in these neighborhoods is a risk factor for health. Decision-makers can be fully aware of problems like this, but avoid needed solutions.

The empathy needed to care about those who are exposed to toxins can be absent. Affected citizens often must inform and motivate leaders to take action for change that can improve people's health. Those who aren't directly affected by these environmental problems can amplify these voices and act as allies. Caring about people and their problems motivates working for change.

There are simple actions you can take to help make the planet healthier for you and others, such as cutting down on how much you buy and throw away, and volunteering with organizations that work to clean up the environment.

Chapter Fourteen

PAYING ATTENTION TO HUMAN BEINGS

UNICEF, a part of the United Nations, has a vision and a goal. The global efforts of the United Nations International Children's Emergency Fund uphold the rights of all children and help every child thrive. Working in more than 190 countries, devoted workers improve the lives of children who are in the greatest need.

Their approach to solving complex problems focuses on human beings and services that fit the needs of real people in the real world. Listening with empathy involves putting aside assumptions and asking questions instead. Investigating and listening create empathy. This also improves communities by creating the services that truly meet the needs of the people.

Meeting the victims of conflict, starvation, disease, and abuse is the human-to-human first step. Workers respond to 96,000 children affected by earthquakes in Afghanistan and food insecurity in Africa. They give aid, comfort, safety, and support to refugees and those in conflict zones. They have the help of donors across the globe and put these resources to work solving problems. Their efforts start with empathy.

Learning from the success of UNICEF in their mission can guide any effort to use empathy to solve problems. Without human-to-human connections and open-minded listening, attempts to make a difference may fall short of a goal. One person can listen to another and understand their experience and their needs. One person can take action that meets the need. Groups large and small can start with genuine empathy and use understanding to build their plan for action.

GLOSSARY

advocacy: The process or act of supporting a certain cause.

ally: One of two or more people or groups who work together.

apathy: A feeling of lacking interest or emotion.

assumption: Something that is believed to be true or is likely true, but is not known to be true.

asthma: A physical condition that makes it hard for someone to breathe.

autism spectrum disorder: A developmental condition usually diagnosed when someone is a child that often causes issues with communicating and forming relationships with others.

bias: To have an unfair preference or dislike of something.

catastrophe: An event or disaster that is extremely or completely terrible.

computer literacy: One's familiarity and level of skill with using computers and applications.

coroner: A public official who works to find out a person's cause of death when it is sudden or violent.

empathy: A feeling that someone deeply understands or shares another's emotions or experiences.

foster: A word that describes the situation in which for a time a child lives with and is cared for by people who are not the child's biological parents.

indifference: A feeling that one lacks interest or concern in something.

initiative: The opportunity or ability to do something before others do it.

isolation: The condition of being alone.

pandemic: An event in which a disease spreads quickly and affects many people over a widespread area, such as the world.

trauma: An experience that is especially difficult or unpleasant and causes someone lasting mental or emotional problems.

INDEX